A CIP catalogue record for this book
is available from the British Library.

ISBN 0-7136-3292-5

A & C Black (Publishers) Limited
35 Bedford Row, London WC1R 4JH

© 1990 Susanna Gretz and Alison Sage

Typeset by Spectrum Typesetting
Printed in Belgium by Proost International Book Production

Teddybears
in trouble

Susanna Gretz & Alison Sage

A & C Black · London

Louise and Charles arrived at the library.
"Stay here, Fred," said Charles.
"We shan't be long."

"Oh good," said Louise.
"*True Stories of Terrible Bears* is back."
"You took that out last time," said Charles.
"It's a good book," said Louise.

"There's a talk on animals today," said Mrs Mullins, the librarian. "You should go, Charles."

They found lots of books about animals.
"There's Dennis," said Louise, "and he's returned his
six books already. He only took them out yesterday."

Dennis looked over Charles' shoulder.
"I've read all those," he said...

"except for the boring ones, like that one."
"That one's mine and it's NOT boring," said Louise.

"I know how to find any book you want," said Dennis.
They went over to the information screen.
"What book shall we look for?" he asked.

"I bet Dennis doesn't know that elephants can't jump,"
said Louise.
"Don't be silly," said Charles,
"Dennis knows all about animals."

"And yak's milk is pink," Louise went on.
"Yak's milk isn't pink," said Dennis.
"It *is*," said Louise.
"Ssh," said Charles, "we're busy."

Louise stomped off and sat at the window.
She didn't feel like reading any more.
Then she looked outside.
Something was missing!

"Fred's gone!" shouted Louise.

"Shhh!" said Dennis.

"Where?" said Charles.

"He's not outside," said Louise.

"He must have followed us into the library."

It's hard looking for a dog in a library;
it's even harder to do it quietly.

Then Louise had an idea.

"You can't go up there," said Dennis.
"You'll fall off."
"No I won't," said Louise.

Louise could see all the way across the library.
It was very full...
but what was that over in the corner?

"Hurry," said Louise,
"Fred wants to join the talk on animals."

Too late! The speaker had already started.

"Dogs learn tricks from their owners,"
said the speaker. "They can't think for themselves."
Fred got off his seat and gave the speaker a book.
"Well!" said the speaker, smiling.
"This is a story about a dog who rescues his family
from a terrible fire. Just a story, I'm afraid."

Fred smelled something good in the speaker's bag.
He took out a packet of biscuits and some papers.
"Whose dog is this?" asked the speaker.

Just then Mrs Mullins appeared.
"Oh no," said Charles.

"Catch him!" yelled Louise,
but Fred was much too quick for them.
Everyone cheered; they thought it was
a special part of the talk.

"I've been doing my best," said the speaker.
Mrs Mullins smiled.
"*What* an interesting talk!" she said.

Charles helped pass the biscuits.
Louise took charge of Fred.
"Can elephants jump?" Louise asked the speaker.
"Oh no," he said. "Their feet are the wrong sort."
"And is yak's milk pink?" asked Dennis.
There was a long pause.

"An interesting question," said the speaker.
"We must look it up."